LOVE IS A BEAST

By

Melody Lynch

Table of Contents

Chapter 1

The buzz of his phone was pissing me off. I laid there and tried to ignore it, but it just kept buzzing. Ryan was in a deep sleep, snoring and all. I picked up my phone to see what time it was. 10 P.M. I tossed the cover off and got out of bed.

I grabbed his phone. It was just a number, no name. I hesitated for a second, but then swiped the green phone, answering the call.

"Hey baby, can you talk?" asked the sultry female voice on the other end. I didn't need to hear anything else this asshole was cheating again.

I threw the cell phone at his face. He jumped up, startled and confused.

"Yolanda, what the fuck? I think you chipped my tooth!" He had his hand pressed against his mouth. I won't lie, I was glad he was hurt.

"Ryan, get the fuck out!" I yelled.

"Yolanda, what are you talking about?"

"The phone, Ryan, the phone."

He picked the phone up and looked at it.

"Hello, hello." The woman was still on the line.

He rolled his eyes and hung it up, and then he laid back in the bed.

"Ryan, I'm not joking you need to leave." he was a fool if he thought he was going to lay beside me after that or maybe I was the fool for always taking him back.

He tossed the cover off and grabbed his shirt and pants from the floor. He was taking his sweet time and it was starting to piss me off.

"Yolanda, if you go looking for some shit, you will find it every time." I wasn't in the mood to hear that bullshit today.

"No Ryan if you were worth a damn, I could look all day and not find anything but yo ass is trifling so you wouldn't understand, just hurry up and get out" I said standing in the doorway with my hands on my hips.

He walked past me with an attitude and a few seconds later I heard the front door open and close. When we first met, I had been taken by his six-foot frame, dark brown eyes, and boy-next-door charm. He made me laugh. We had come from similar backgrounds; my mother was emotionally unavailable and his dad had walked out on their family. I thought that would bring us together and help us break the cycle but I had been dead wrong. I should have left the first time he cheated, but here we are.

I peeked out the blinds and watched as he got in his car and shut the door. I could see the glow from the cell phone, so he had called whoever she was back.

I sat on the bed and cried. Five years down the drain, this time, I had to admit that Ryan would never stop cheating, so either I had to end it, this time for real, or go through the rest of the relationship knowing my heart and ph balance would always be broken. I didn't have any girlfriends to call and vent to, so I had to nurse this hurt alone.

I pulled my silk nightgown off and pulled on a t-shirt and a pair of sweats. I needed a drink, and if I hurried, I could make it to the corner store and grab two bottles of wine before they closed. I slid my feet into a pair of slides and was out the door. I hustled inside the grimy corner store and tossed two bottles of cheap wine on the counter.

"Long night?" the cashier asked.

"The longest."

He rang me up and handed me my change.

I held my brown bag close to me and started home. When I was almost there, I saw a group of people huddled in front of my building, shooting dice. I saw them out here from time to time, always wearing matching outfits. I figured they were out here hustling, but that was their business, so I walked by them as quickly as I could.

None of them looked my way. I went inside and locked the door behind me. I pulled my wine glass from the shelf and cracked open the first bottle.

The cheap wine was gross, but it was better than nothing. Before I knew it, I had downed the entire bottle and had my eyes on the second.

On some level, I wasn't even that hurt, for real. After so many times it hurt for a little while and then it just went numb, it was still there, aching and festering made me look at the ground ashamed or wondering what each woman had that I didn't. I had been there to nurse his pain and I walked with him when he didn't have anything so why didn't that matter? I was done with love. From here on out, I'd fuck 'em and keep it moving. I had rocked like that when I was in college, and it had served me just fine. I had a ton of fun and didn't waste one second walking around heartbroken. I smiled at the thought but I knew I was fooling myself. I wasn't built like that anymore.

I poured the wine that was in my cup down in the sink. I walked into the bathroom and turned on the hot water. It felt good against my skin, washing away the stress of the day. I lathered up with my favorite body soap and traced soft circles around my breast, then squeezed my nipples. The heavy pressure between my legs reminded me of how long it had been since I had some release, which should have been a red flag. I rinsed off and took extra time toweling off and putting on lotion. I slid into my lacy red bra and panties.

I laid down on the bed. The sheets were cool against my back. I slid my hand under my bralette and traced circles across my nipples. I slid a hand under my panties, running a finger over my throbbing clit.

"Ayo, my man?" A man was talking loud as hell right outside my window.

Damn. I can't even take some pressure off because these clowns outside were being loud.

The pressure mixed with the cheap wine had me pissed. I jumped out of bed and pulled on a t-shirt and sweatpants. I swung the door open and jogged down the steps.

I walked over toward the group, who were all bent over, still shooting dice.

"Excuse me, could you guys keep it down?"

They all whipped around and looked at me.

A tall man with a head full of waves stood up and stepped toward me. He had a long, jagged scar that ran from the top of his head to the bottom of his jaw, but he was still handsome.

"Sorry about that, ma." That apology wasn't good enough, and why was his fresh butt calling me ma I had to be at least ten years older than him

"Some of us have work in the morning," I shot back, blowing off his half-assed apology.

"Yo, Precious, come check this sadity bitch." Me and my big mouth had got me into some shit.

A brown-skinned twenty something chick wearing a flannel shirt and leggings barreled toward me. She had a nice size on her and she was smiling, I knew she wasn't going to be yelling and talking she was coming over here to brawl.

She threw a hard punch that burst my lip. Copper-flavored blood poured into my mouth.

The young men standing around watched and laughed. I dodged her next punch and threw an uppercut that rocked her head back. She shook it off and stepped toward me, but I threw a few quick wild punches. She fell down, and I stepped back instead of pouncing on her.

The men started circling around, closed in on me. i knew these young dudes don't have a problem jumping a woman so I prayed that it would be quick.

"Yo, what the fuck are ya'll doing?" a voice boomed. The group parted and a man walked through wearing a tan leather jacket, cargo pants, and dark Timberlands. He had to be at least 6'2", with broad shoulders and wavy hair. He had dark ebony skin and a low fade.

"I'm going to ask one more time...what are y'all doing?"

"Raheem, we were just out here checking this bitch who came out here tripping'," Precious said as she got off the pavement and dusted herself off.

That's when his eyes landed on me. They were dark brown, but for a brief second, they flashed yellow...and then I knew I had drunk too much.

I put my hand up to my nose because I felt the blood trickle down.

"Sorry about that, ma'am," he said. His bottom teeth were covered in diamonds.

"Whatever, just keep it down." I tried to keep a shred of dignity as I marched back towards my building and up the steps holding my nose. I slammed the door behind me and locked it.

I grabbed a paper towel and plugged my nose up and then I snatched the bottle of wine from the table and went back to my room. I sat back on the edge of my bed and took a big swig. I can't believe I took my behind out there tripping going on out there to confront them had been dumb as hell. I could have lost my life and the truth is they hadn't even been that loud I had just picked a fight.

"What are y'all thinking out here fighting with a human?" his voice was low and there was anger bubbling behind it.

What was he talking about? I leaned closer to the window.

"We have a fuckin' job to do. What we are out here doing is way more important than that petty shit"

"You right, Raheem, sorry," Precious said.

After that, it was quiet. I sat the bottle down and laid back on my bed. This cheap wine had me all messed up in the head.

Chapter 2

The next day, as soon as I walked into the house, I kicked off my shoes and took my blazer off. I was a licensed counselor and operated my private practice, but I hated it. They had warned us about burnout in college, but I had blown it off. It wasn't until I was in the field that I realized how draining it was, to help people work through their trauma day after day. It left me feeling mentally exhausted most days. If I hadn't racked up so much student loan debt, I would have changed careers in a heartbeat. I would still help people. Just not sitting in an office trying to work through their issues.

I walked to the fridge and yanked it open. An expired jug of milk and a container of old lunch meat stared back at me.

Damn, I need to go grocery shopping. I slammed the refrigerator door shut. There was a knock on the door. I never have company. Hell, I work too much to have friends, and if it's Ryan with a half-assed apology, he's got another thing coming. I marched to the door and yanked it open, but it wasn't Ryan. It was the man from last night. Damn, he was fine in the daytime. He had a firm jaw and thick, brown lips.

"Hey, ma'am. How are you doing?"

I put my hands on my hips. Did he come here to try to intimidate me?

"My name is Yolanda."

"I just wanted to stop by and tell you again how sorry I am about last night." He pulled a bouquet of Roses from behind his back, and pushed them toward me, and then he sneezed. It was a lite cute sneeze, not something I expected from this towering man in front of me so it made me smile.

"Thank you for the flowers, but you didn't have to do this." I reached out and took them from him. No man had ever gotten me flowers, I wasn't even sure if I liked flowers but the gesture had me feeling all warm on the inside.

" I'm Raheem. As an apology, would it be okay if I took you to dinner?"

I had not been expecting that. I thought he had more sinister motives.

"No thanks. I'm about to cook." The lie left my lips before I truly thought the offer through.

"Okay, well, maybe another time then," he said, flashing that damn smile at me. He turned around and walked down the steps. I watched him walk away still full of swagger and confidence. It was sexy as hell besides why was I sitting here playing coy when my dog-ass ex had been spreading it around the whole five years we had been together?

I jogged down the steps and called out to him.

"Raheem, on second thought, I would like to go to dinner."

He turned around and walked back to me. When he was in front of me, I had to look up at him. I caught a whiff of his cologne. It smelled so good.

"Do you mind just giving me some time to get dressed? I just got off work."

"No problem, beautiful. See you in, what, an hour?" Beautiful? This man was laying it on thick but I can't lie he was smooth with it.

"Yes, that will be fine."

"Alright I'll be here to pick you up" he said before he turned and walked down the sidewalk. I had to shake some sense into myself so I wouldn't stand there and watch him walk away. I was acting like a horny teenager. I had dated a few men in my day so I wasn't a prude but there was an energy that radiated from him that just did something to me.

An hour later, I was showered and dressed to impress. I wore a cami maxi dress that hugged all the right places and had a thigh-high split that gave just enough sass. My braids were old, but they looked fine once I slapped some gel on my edges. I put in my gold hoops, stepped into my strappy black heels, and was ready. I gave myself a once over in the mirror and smiled. Who said that almost thirty was old? Because tonight I was bringing it.

I paced around the living room and put on some lip-gloss. What if he stood me up and never came?

But all that faded away when the two knocks on the door came. I smiled, ready for him to see me out of my work clothes. but this time, it was Ryan. He was holding his gym bag like he planned to stay a while.

He looked me up and down. "Where are you going?" I wanted to roll my eyes. He had some nerve.

"No, Ryan, the correct question is, what are you doing here?" Did he think I was supposed to be sitting at home crying? Probably, since that's what I had done all the times before.

"Yolanda, you know how we do. I'm a man. I fuck around sometimes, but I always come home to you. I love you." He took a step closer and gave me those sad puppy dog eyes. There was a time in my life I would have done anything for this man. I thought he was God's gift to me but the whole time he was a devil in disguise.

"Ryan what does love matter if it won't keep you out of other women's beds?"

But before he could answer, a black Yukon on big rims pulled up. Raheem jumped out, but when he saw what was going on, he stood back and watched. I couldn't help but smile when I saw him.

I turned back to Ryan, "Ryan, you can go back to wherever you've been. We are over." He sucked his teeth and disbelief flashed across his eyes as I walked down the stairs past him. After five years of him dogging me out, I'm sure he thought I would never leave.

"Late on the first date. Not a good look," I said as I walked up to Raheem.

"Sorry about that, beautiful." He kissed my cheek and walked me to the passenger side door, opening it for me. I slid inside and sat back. I wished I could see the look on Ryan's face.

"Thanks for playing along," I said when we pulled out of the lot.

"What do you mean?"

"Well, this isn't a date, is it?"

"It's whatever you want it to be." He sat back in the driver's seat and gripped the steering wheel with one hand. The other rested on top of his thigh. I grinned and looked out the window as we pulled out of the parking spot and down the street. I wondered what I was getting myself into?

We drove to the industrial side of the neighborhood. We pulled up in front of an old textile factory that had been closed down for years. I got a little nervous. Maybe this had been some type of setup to get me back for what I had done to Precious the other night. I mean, I watch crime TV. I know they do shit like this sometimes.

He used the palm of his hand to control the wheel while he looked over his shoulder to parallel park. He got out and walked over to open my door. He held his hand out to help me out of the trunk but he didn't let it go. We walked side by side toward the old building. I couldn't help but think that I should have brought my mace just in case something crazy was about to go down. When he opened the door, my mind was blown. Someone had completely renovated the inside of. The refinished brick walls were exposed. The terracotta ceilings were beautiful. The string lights gave the place a chill vibe.

There was a young woman behind the hostess station. She smiled at us when we walked in. "Good evening, and welcome to The Den."

"Reservation for Raheem." he had really planned this out like he knew the whole time that I would agree to go out with him.

She glanced down at a sheet of paper. "Certainly. Follow me."

While we followed behind her, I looked around, taking it all in. People were sitting at the stylish wooden tables, drinking beer and eating. We walked past a beautiful marble bar with wooden framed mirrors and shelves. Our table was at the very back of the restaurant.

"What can I get you two to drink?"

"Double shot of Hennessy. No ice."

The waitress looked at me. "And for the lady?"

"I'll have the same."

Raheem raised an eyebrow but didn't say anything. I wasn't a huge liquor drinker, but I liked a nice cocktail from time to time.

"This place is beautiful. I have never seen anything like it," I gushed after the hostess walked off.

"I'm glad you like it. I'll let my brother know he did a good job with it."

"What do you mean? He did the design?"

"No, he owns it." I noticed his eyes were scanning the restaurant. He watched whenever someone laughed too loud or banged against a chair. I see this sometimes with some of my clients who have Post Traumatic Stress Disorder. But this didn't work, so I needed to stop trying to analyze him.

"No way, really?"

"Yeah, a lot of the people who work here are felons.' People nobody else would hire. My brother thinks we should buy back the block and put money into these old buildings—repurposing them into restaurants, grocery stores, and shit like that."

The waitress came back and set our drinks down.

"You don't agree?" I asked as I sipped my drink. The brown liquor burned the entire way down. Maybe I should have opted for wine.

"Yeah, I do, but I been trying to tell my brother these streets don't love nobody. You can do everything for these people out here, and they will still snake you out."

I swear his eyes turned yellow for a second. I set the drink down and pushed it away. Maybe I should have ordered water, because alcohol has not been agreeing with me lately.

"So, Yolanda, tell me more about yourself."

The conversation and the drinks flowed. By the time we were done, I knew he had an older brother named Elijah, and both of their parents had been killed when they were young, but they had some family here and there. Elijah had worked a bunch of jobs until he had enough money to get into real estate. Raheem took a little longer to let go of the street life, but he eventually followed suit. He explained that the group I saw him with was an intervention program he led. They tried to keep dudes from taking their beef to the next level, but sometimes the intervention crew could get a little rowdy themselves. I thought it was admirable.

I told him my story—how I came from a single home with a depressed mom and lots of toxic family drama. That's why I had become a counselor—I thought I could learn how to fix not just me and my family but other people, too. But, as a first-generation college student with no guidance, I made a bunch of mistakes and took out a bunch of loans, and now that I had the career I dreamed of, it left me feeling defeated every day. I had not intended to drop my whole life story on him but the Hennessy had made my tongue loose, but Raheem didn't seem to mind. He was the type of person who listened with their eyes watching the whole time, never interrupting or trying to make it about himself.

When the check came, he tipped generously, which I appreciated because I like a man who treats all people with respect, and showing gratitude to people in customer service roles was a huge plus.

When we were back in the truck, I rolled my window down. The cool air felt good on my face.

"Yolanda, do you dance?" he asked as we pulled up in front of my place.

"I can do a little something." The truth was I hadn't been to a club or danced in years. Silverton wasn't the same. You couldn't just go out and club hop and have a good time these days. A fun night could lead to drama.

"Next time, we'll go dancing then."

I was cheesing, happy that there would be a next time. Maybe he knew of a nice jazz lounge or something where they only allowed grown folks.

He walked me to the door and, like the gentleman he was, kissed me on the cheek. His lips were full and soft.

"Thank you for coming out with me Yolanda. I had a great time," I knew that I didn't want the night to end.

"Raheem, how about a nightcap?"

"I thought you would never ask. His face lit up and he smiled. I unlocked the door and we walked in.

"Make yourself at home" I said as I walked into the kitchen.

He walked in and looked around. "Oh, so you like art?"

"Yes, these are a few pieces I scored in college. I could barely afford noodles, but I got art."

He smiled and sat on the sofa while I went to the kitchen and poured two glasses of wine.

When I handed him a glass, he pretended to be a connoisseur, sniffing an exquisite blend.

"You got jokes, I see." I sat next to him. It was crazy how comfortable I was with him. Being around him was easy.

"What kind of music did you get in here?"

I handed him the remote to the tv and let him scroll through my digital playlist.

I sipped my wine and looked at him over the glass. I had dated my fair share of men, but there was something different about Raheem. He thought before he spoke plus, he was the perfect gentleman with the right amount of grit. It's almost like he was too good to be true.

A song came on that I instantly recognized.

"This is my song!" I sat my glass on the end table and stood up. "Get up and dance with me."

He pushed himself off the couch and joined me on the makeshift dance floor. Our bodies swayed to the beat. He pulled me close and I grinded my body against him, He firmly gripped my hips. It sent shivers through me. I bit my lip and closed my eyes as I wondered what his hands would feel like on other parts of my body.

A commercial came on, interrupting the entire vibe. I cursed myself for being cheap and not spending the money on the premium subscription.

We both laughed at the interruption.

He crashed on the couch and grabbed me by the arm, pulling me down on top of him. Heat radiated off him and wrapped around me like a blanket. I laid my head on his chest and listened to the drum of his heartbeat while he ran his fingers through the parts in my braids. An old R&b song came on. The male singer had a smooth falsetto. He could sing the panties off of a woman.

I sat up, and Raheem was looking at me. It felt like he was looking right into my soul.

He grabbed the back of my neck and kissed me. I could taste the wine on his tongue as it explored mine. I would not hold back. I had never wanted a person so badly. If it was a one-night stand, then so be it.

I stood up and grabbed him by the hand leading him into my bedroom. We crashed against the wall, hungry for each other. He took his shirt off. His muscles were chiseled, and he had tattoos on both arms. I stepped out of my dress. He looked me up and down and licked his lips. He sat on the bed and leaned back on his elbows. I slowly walked over to him and he drank me in with his eyes. I felt like the sexiest woman on the planet.

I unbuckled his pants and released his manhood. It had to be nine inches long and thick. He was rock hard, and the veins on his dick pulsed.

I climbed on top of him and unfastened my bra. He took my breast in his hand and traced his thumb across my nipple. While he grabbed the back of my neck with his other hand, it sent tingles down my spine.

I pulled back and pulled my panties to the side. I grinded up and down against him. He moaned but it sounded more like a growl. I lowered myself on top of him, the tip of his dick spread my slippery lips apart. I eased myself down onto him slowly, enjoying every inch. He grabbed my hips and guided me up and down. Together, we found a rhythm. I felt the jolts of a powerful orgasm building up.

He grabbed my face. "Don't close your eyes. I want to watch you cum."

I looked him in the eyes as we rocked in sync. He gripped my hips hard until I climaxed. I cried out as waves of pleasure ripped through me.

Raheem flipped me over and slid into me from behind. I was soaking wet, but he still stretched my walls. The hard, full feeling felt so damn good. I arched my hips and threw my ass back while I used a finger to rub soft circles around my clit. Each stroke brought me closer to another orgasm.

"Raheem, please don't stop," I gasped and gripped the sheets. My body locked up as a gush of warm liquid released from my pussy.

"Oh, shit. I'm about to cum," he moaned. His grip on my hips tightened, and his thrusts sped up and then stopped as he filled me up.

His cum dripped down my thighs. I collapsed on the bed. He laid next to me.

I tried to catch my breath. Tiny currents of electricity shot through my body.

"Are you okay?" He reached over and rubbed my back, but that made the sensation more intense, so I wiggled away from him. It took a few minutes for me to feel normal.

"I have seen girls do that in porn, but I didn't think it was real," he said. His eyes were gleaming.

"Guess we were each other's first, because I've never done that before"

He laughed and kissed me on the mouth.

The following day, I walked out of the bathroom after a shower. Raheem had stayed the night and was sitting on the side of the bed, fully dressed.

"Yolonda, I need to ask you something."

"Don't worry, I'm on the pill," I said as I tied my robe closed.

He smiled. "Well, that's good to know, but that's not it. I need to know if last night was just to get back at your ex."

I hadn't thought about Ryan since I left him standing on my porch. It was a surprise since we had been together for five years.

"No, it wasn't to get back. It just felt right." Heat rushed to my cheeks. I felt corny telling this to a man I had just met.

He stood up and wrapped his arms around me.

"Good, because you're mine now."

I relaxed into his arms.

Chapter 3

It was Saturday. I was in the back of a cab headed to the Hope for the East is a community outreach center. I had interned there years ago and I had a soft spot for the place. I stopped by whenever I could to volunteer or give referrals. I admired the founder, Karina. She jumped through hoops for her clients and treated them respectfully, even if they were struggling with addiction or mental health issues.

Karina was standing at the printer when I walked in. "Yolanda! I didn't know you were coming in today." She looked tired but happy to see me.

"Hey, Karina. I came down to see if you all needed some help today." I walked over and sat down at the round table. This side of the building is where all the admin stuff happens. Long phone calls with social workers, deal-brokering for housing programs, a lot of blood, sweat, and tears happened here.

"Yolanda, you know we love having you here. I wish I could afford to pay you to come on full time."

She grabbed the papers from the tray. "Can I get you a cup of coffee?"

"Sure," I said as I tried to get comfortable in my seat.

Karina walked over to the old coffee pot and grabbed a paper cup.

"Yolanda, I wanted to thank you again for getting that referral for Suzanne. Her son is doing much better now that his new psychiatrist got his meds lined out." She walked over and sat the cup of coffee in front of me. I picked it up and blew at it.

"I'm glad he is doing better," I said before I took a sip of the coffee. It always made my eyes water; it was so bitter, but the boost from the caffeine was unmatched. I looked up at Karina; she had big bags under her eyes.

"Karina, how are things really? It looks like you haven't been sleeping." She smiled at me. Karina was one of those people who took care of everyone except herself.

"The landlord is talking about selling this building; I have been stressing about where we would move the center too. "I wish we could get one of those grants. I have been applying for years, but no luck yet."

I sat there sipping my coffee, wishing that there was something I could do. This center helped so people and the community would suffer if it had to close its doors.

"Alright that's enough of me complaining. So, if you're ready, we got a lot of hungry people out there."

"Let's do it," I said.

We were behind the buffet counter handing out lunch for today's clients. The stove in the kitchen had gone out, so while Karina figured out how she was going to get the money to replace it, we were handing out sack lunches.

The line was long, but it flew by. Bessie Mae was the last person in line. She was in her sixties, with thin black hair. She stood sort of hunched over, but she was smart as a whip and hilarious. Sometimes she wore her dentures, and sometimes she didn't. Today she had decided not to.

"Nice to see you, stranger."

"Hey, Ms. Bessie."

"Child, I have told you just to call me Bessie."

I smiled and nodded my head. Even at my age it was hard to call one of my elders by their first name.

"Come, have a seat with me," she said as I handed her a brown bag.

Since she was the last person in line, I had a few minutes before I had to help Karina clean-up for the evening. I followed her to the table and pulled out a chair. She picked through the bag, pushed her sandwich to the side, and opted for the bright-orange.

"What's been going on, Ms. Thang?" she said as she peeled the fruit.

"Not much, just working."

She nodded her head. "Umm-hmm. You got that new man glow." She plopped a piece of the orange in her mouth and started smashing it with her gums. I blushed because I didn't think it was that obvious that something new was going on with me.

"Bessie, where are your dentures? Do you need a referral for a new pair?"

"Girl, I wasn't fooling with them thangs today," she said, giving me a gummy smile. I started cracking up.

I saw Karina walking toward the buffet center with a trash can.

"Alright, Bessie, I'm going to help Karina clean up."

"Alright, baby. Take care of yourself."

"Bessie, have you thought anymore about applying for housing again?"

She swallowed her fruit and swept the peel off the table before she looked at me.

"Baby, you know I'm not begging them people down there for nothing. I live on my own terms." A lady named Mary Anne walked over to the table "Bessie girl lets go get a nip" she said in a hushed voice.

I smiled and stood up from the table

"Mary girl, go over there and wait for me by the door," she said. Mary Anne did as she was told

Bessie stood up and looked at me. "Yolanda baby I told you before you better stop trying to save the world and live ya life," she walked over to Mary Anne and the two of them walked out of the center.

Karina walked over to me. "Still got a soft spot for Bessie, huh?"

"Yeah. I just wish she would straighten up." I tried getting her housing referrals, but she would never take them.

"We can't save them all," she patted me on the back and walked off.

Chapter 4

$\mathbf{M}$e and Raheem were in the kitchen making lunch together. He had just taken the skillet off the stove and sprinkled the sauce on the vegetables for the stir-fry we were making.

"So, what had you so busy yesterday?" Raheem asked as he put the vegetables on a plate. He didn't have a shirt on, and he was wearing a pair of gray sweatpants. I bit my lip and tried to push down my dirty thoughts. It really was nice to spend this type of time with someone.

"A couple of Saturdays out of the month. I volunteer at Hope for the East"

He turned around and looked at me. "Really?"

"Yeah. I interned there when I was in college. I still go down and help and give referrals when I can." he stood there looking at me.

"That place does great work. Next time you go, is it okay if I tag along?" he asked

I just stared at him, lost for words.

"I mean, if you don't want me to, that's okay, too."

That's when I realized that I probably had a confused look on my face. "No, no, I definitely want you to come. But you gone have to put on an apron, no standing around." I pulled a bottle of wine from the rack.

"Of course. Ya boy knows how to rattle some pots."

I laughed and walked over to the cabinet to grab a wine glass.

"So, what's your favorite meal?"

He walked over and wrapped his arms around me. He placed warm, wet kisses on the back of my neck.

"You." he said before he bent me over the counter.

Chapter 5

I was sitting in my office, thumbing through a stack of papers on my desk. My secretary Ashley walked in, "Here you go," she said as she handed me a thick stack of past due invoices. She stood there like she was going to say something but thought better of it before she walked out. My prices were based on a sliding scale, but even then, many of my clients couldn't afford to pay but they needed help so I couldn't turn them away. But if things kept going like this, I wouldn't be able to keep the office lights on much longer. I sat there rubbing my temples when my cell phone rang. My mother's name popped on the screen. I hesitated for a moment but answered.

"Hello?"

"Yolanda, can you send me some money? I need to put something on this high ass utility bill."

"Well, hello to you too, Ma. Yeah, I can send you some money. How are you doing?"

"Well, you know. My sugar has been sky high; doctors won't do anything about it. Just tell me how to cook. I know how to cook. Been cooking damn near my whole life."

"They know nothing, anyway." I pushed the stack of envelopes to the corner of my desk. I've seen this play out since I was a little girl—ma would go to the doctor, they would tell her what's wrong, and she would do the complete opposite. I wasn't in the mood to push the issue today, so I changed the subject.

"Ma, I have someone that I want you to meet."

"Yolanda, I've already met that pretty boy Ryan. What's the big deal?

"Ma, me and Ryan broke up weeks ago. If you answered your phone sometimes, you would know that." My mother had been like that since I was a little girl. She would go into these deep depressions and cut contact with everyone, sometimes for months at a time.

"Girl, he probably broke up with you cuz you done gained all that weight. You know a man like something pretty to look at when he home from work."

I started rubbing my temples because I knew where this conversation was going. "Ma, even if I gained some weight, that's no reason to cheat."

"Yolanda, they're men; that's what they do. Long as they pay the bills and come home to you, no big deal."

"Ma, I pay my own bills."

"Okay, Mrs. Independent. That's why you never gone get a husband."

I regretted the fact that I had answered her call.

"So, what restaurant are you wanting to go to?"

"The new Mexican place off 10th street," I said, happy that she seemed open to the idea of Raheem even if she had to take a few shots at me first.

"That place that has all those fools waiting outside for hours?"

"Yeah, ma, that's the one. But don't worry, Raheem can get us reservations."

"Raheem, huh? Girl, I can't afford that place, Yolanda. You know my check ain't but seven hundred dollars—"

"Ma, I'm not asking you to pay for anything. I'm just saying come out and have dinner with us!"

"Alright, I'll be there. Just tell me what time."

Three days later.

We were sitting on the patio of the Mexican restaurant. The sun was blazing. Raheem had his hand on my thigh. It was hot out here, so I opted for a tank top, midi skirt, and pumps. My mom and I had a complicated relationship, but I was glad he was finally going to meet her. Ever since I was a little girl, I dreamed about having this huge close-knit family, with a husband and three babies hanging off their grandmother. And with Raheem, I felt like that could be a real possibility.

I picked up the phone and dialed my mom to see if she had gotten lost. We had already been waiting forty-five minutes. It went straight to voicemail. Raheem used his free hand to tuck a braid behind my ear.

Twenty minutes later, the waitress came back and asked if we were ready to order. It took everything I had to keep the tears from falling. She wasn't coming, and she didn't even have the decency to call and say anything.

Raheem sent the waitress away.

"Can we just go home?" I whispered. I was embarrassed and hurt.

He put his hand under my chin and lifted my head. "Keep your head up, Yolanda." I was able to blink back the tears. Raheem settled the tab, and we got in the truck to head home. I wasn't in the best of moods, and it still pissed me at the way my mom had ghosted me.

When we got to the house, I went straight to the kitchen and chugged a glass of wine. I poured another, and then I flopped down on the sofa. My mother had her struggles my entire life—I just wished for once she could have shown up for me. But if she couldn't even be bothered to attend my college graduation, I should have known better. I felt pathetic—a grown woman still crying about her mommy not showing up. I took a big gulp from the wineglass. I was going to need another bottle. I just wanted to numb the pain and not feel anything.

Raheem came and sat beside me. He tapped my leg and motioned for me to put it on his lap. when he was settled, he started to stroke my leg. My eyes were puffy from crying, but his touch felt good and calmed the sad storm brewing inside of me.

"Baby, I wanted to do this at the restaurant," he said as he pulled something from his back pocket. "Yolonda, you work hard as hell. I watch you come home every day without the weight of the world on your shoulders from trying to save everybody."

I sat up, wondering what Raheem had up his sleeve.

"Baby, I don't know what's going on with your mom, but that's not your cross to carry. You have come too far for that, and I want you to chase your dreams no matter what." He handed me an envelope.

I ran my finger across the envelope and stared at him.

"Come on, open it up," he urged.

I ran my finger under the seal and opened the envelope. It was a check made out to the student loan department.

I put my hand on my chest and ugly cried , but they were tears of happiness. I wrapped my arms around him, and he squeezed me.

"I got your back, Yolanda. I mean that."

Chapter 6

Baby, when are you going to introduce me to your brother?"

He sucked his teeth. "Yolanda, Elijah is busy. I barely see him unless it's about business."

It didn't make any sense. If they were so close, wouldn't Elijah be curious about who his little brother was spending so much time with?

"Raheem, are you ashamed of me? Is there another woman?" Lately, my intuition had been telling me that something was off; I didn't feel like a part of his real life. I wanted to know who his friends were. What was his family get-together like? I didn't have that, so I wanted to see what it was like through Raheem.

He gripped the steering wheel tighter. "Yolanda, I would break it off before I cheated."

"Then damn, what is it? Why are you hiding me, or what are you hiding from me?"

"Yolanda, can we do this when we get home?"

I sat back and folded my arms against my chest. I was pouting like a little girl, but I couldn't help it. We had intertwined every other part of our life. We shared our money and our bodies, so what was the secret?

When we got home, I stomped around, giving him the silent treatment. Petty, I know, but I'm only human. When it was time for bed, I put my bonnet on and rolled up in all the covers.

The mattress creaked as Raheem got out of bed.

When I turned to see where he was going, he had sat on the edge of the bed. He had his head in his hands.

"Yolanda, me and my family are not like everyone else."

"I know that, Raheem." He was constantly reminding me he and his brother were different.

"You don't understand."

"Don't you trust me by now?"

He exhaled, and I felt bad because he looked defeated. It was hard to explain my need to have an intact family to Raheem. My mom and extended family were toxic, so I longed to have a family. I knew if he would just let me meet his brother, Elijah would love me.

"We aren't human."

I screwed my face up. I knew it was too good to be true. There had to be something wrong with him, and now I know what it was: he's crazy as hell!

"What are you then, Raheem?" I rolled my eyes because I knew it was about to be some nonsense.

"Werewolves."

I did not just hear this man say he was a werewolf.

His shoulders slumped. Raheem had a sense of humor, but this was wild, even for him.

"Werewolves, like in Little Red Riding Hood?" I couldn't hold it in. I started cracking up.

He stood up and looked at me. His eyes glowed a bright yellow.

I stopped laughing. I remembered I had seen his eyes turn yellow the first time we had dinner, but I'd thought I was drunk and tripping. My heart crashed against my chest.

There was a popping sound, and his muscles twitched and bulged under his skin.

His nose cracked, and his jaws stretched until his mouth contorted into a muzzle. He threw his head back, and long, sharp teeth cut through his gums. He held up his hands, and one by one, his fingers snapped backward and curved into knifelike claws. It replaced his beautiful brown skin with smoky gray fur.

I passed out.

When I came to, Raheem was holding me. Raheem, the man, not the werewolf.

I scrambled away from him and ran to the corner.

"I would never hurt you." He sat on the bed, and a tear fell down his face. " Yolanda, being what I am, has taken so much from me. I would never hurt you. But I won't keep secrets from you."

He looked defeated. I knew this man was strong—this man who held me softly in his arms and listened to me cry about everything from work to my mother. I never had anyone reciprocate my love the way he did. I never had to question anything he said because his actions spoke louder than any words ever could.

I took a breath and walked over to him. He wrapped his arms around my waist and rested his face against my belly.

I kissed the top of his head. "Raheem, did you mean it when you said I was yours?"

"Yes."

"Well, it's going to take more than that to get rid of me." It was a lot to take in. Not only were werewolves real, but I was madly in love with one. I didn't know if I had lost my entire mind, but I knew I didn't want to lose Raheem.

He chuckled and squeezed me tighter.

The next few weeks were tense as I tried to get comfortable, but eventually, I came to think of his wolf like a birthmark—one that I knew was there. But never had to see.

I asked him lots of questions about what it meant to be a werewolf. Sometimes he would answer, and sometimes he wouldn't. Certain things, like how the pack handled their business or how they had stayed hidden for so long, were off-limits. One night over dinner, I asked him if Bigfoot was real. He laughed and said that there were a lot of creatures that humans didn't know about.

So, I asked the next obvious question. "Are vampires real?"

His eyes glowed yellow, and his body tensed up with anger.

I got an icy chill down my spine and decided I would not ask any more questions.

Whenever I went out by myself, I was paranoid and always looked over my shoulder. I didn't think anything was after me, but to be on this earth all these years and then learn that everything that went bump in the night was real was scary.

I was glad Raheem trusted me with the truth, but I also wished he had kept it a secret. Did I love him? Yes. But did I flinch when he got too angry? Yes.

Chapter 7

A year later.

You know what, Raheem? I'm tired of your excuses." I threw a pillow hard at his face. "We've been together for a year, and I still haven't met anyone in your family. Not your brother or a cousin."

"Yolanda, I've told you now is not a good time."

"When's it going to be right?" My hands were on my hips. He had told me he was a werewolf, so what could be bigger than that?

"Yolanda, if this is the only thing you have to complain about, shouldn't you be happy I'm not out here cheating like your ex?"

"Fuck you, Raheem. For all I know, your ex could be one of these strays running around the block."

Yes, I had lost my mind. Insulting a werewolf and comparing him to a damn dog. Something had changed between us. The way he could be so nonchalant really pissed me off, and I felt like I had to do something huge to get his attention. Yea, it was childish. Raheem had been spending more time away from the house. He was being more secretive; his phone stayed silent, and he kept it face down. We barely had sex. I had been through this too many times before. I knew he was cheating.

"Yolanda, I'm not doing this right now,"

"Then when Raheem? Huh? Next full moon?" I couldn't control myself. I usually treated Raheem with the utmost respect, but I was sick of his bullshit. Walking around like nothing bothered him.

He walked up to me, his eyes yellow. His shoulders hunched up. "Yolanda, a lot is going on right now in the pack, stuff I can't tell you about; you need to believe that this is my attempt at keeping you safe.

I never thought Raheem would hurt me, but this time, I had crossed the line. I took a step back from him, and the yellow flickered out of his eyes.

"Yolanda, I don't know what your problem is. I have given you everything you claimed you wanted. You know my family situation is complicated, but you keep digging and digging. Have you ever thought that you wouldn't be safe around my family? That maybe I'm trying to protect you?"

"Raheem, I don't need protecting."

I sucked my teeth at the audacity of him, trying to wiggle out of the situation like I was stupid.

"Raheem, don't make shit up. I know you are cheating. Just man up or wolf up and admit it." I knew I was being unreasonable, but the rage was surging through me.

His muscles twitched under his shirt. He threw his hands up in the air. "This shit is over." he walked into the bedroom and grabbed his overnight bag. He started picking up all his clothes and stuffing them in the bag.

"Raheem, are you serious right now? So, it gets hard and you bounce." The tears were rolling down my face. I knew I looked weak, and I hated it, but I didn't want him to leave, especially not like this.

"Yolanda, I can't give you what you need, the big happy family with the doting Mom and brother-in-law. You deserve that and I wished I could give it to you but I can't."

He grabbed his keys from the counter and slammed the door behind him. I knew it was over because Raheem never made empty threats.

I grabbed a glass from the end table and threw it against the wall. I cried and felt sorry for myself. I laid in bed, wrapped up in the comforter that still smelled like him. I cried until my eyes were puffy and no more tears would come. A few hours later I was sitting on the sofa, watching a ratchet reality show, trying to make myself feel better about my mess of a life. Just as two of the main characters were about to fight, there was a knock at the door. I rushed over hoping that Raheem reconsidered. I yanked the door open, ready to jump in his arms. But it was three police officers all wearing tactical vests, one in the front and two in the back, were all holding big guns.

"Search warrant." He shoved a piece of paper at me.

One officer pointed his gun at me. "You sit on the couch"

I walked over to the couch and sat down. My legs felt like noodles.

"Where is Raheem Santers?" the officer in front barked; they didn't wait for an answer, they just started ripping things apart. I watched as they went into the bedroom and tossed things out of the drawer.

"The officers walked into the front room and stood in front of me. "Do you know the penalty for harboring a werewolf?"

"I didn't know it was illegal," I stammered.

"But you knew he was a werewolf?" another one asked.

I felt clammy. Everything was happening so fast, and I couldn't get my thoughts together.

"Yes, he told me what he was."

"Did he ever show you?"

"Yeah, he did. He showed me his wolf once." Damn, was I supposed to say that?

"Where are the rest of them, and who is their leader?"

"I don't know." It was the truth.

"You could go away for a long time. These werewolves are a national threat."
I put my head in my hands and cried. I had never even had a speeding ticket, but I was about to go to jail all for someone who had walked out on me.

"The only thing that's going to help you is telling us everything we need to know."

I wiped my eyes and sat up. "Ok, I don't know much; he didn't talk about their business often."

"Did he ever mention any of the other wolves by name?"

"Only his brother Elijah." The officer nodded his head.

"Does he have any belongings here?"

My eyes darted around the house. He had taken all of his clothes and shoes when he broke up with me earlier.

I shrugged my shoulders. "He might have left a toothbrush."

All the officers looked at each other, and two of them ran off toward the bathroom. A few seconds later, one of them yelled out, "bingo." He walked into the front room and dropped the toothbrush in a plastic baggie. Then they all rushed out.

I sat on the couch, trying to get control of my breath. My hands were shaking and my heart was running a million miles a minute. After I had calmed myself down, I looked for the warrant to see if there was any information on what the hell was going on. I saw it on the floor next to the front door, and when I bent down and picked it up, I felt the blood drain out of my face. It was blank.

Chapter 8

The next morning, I was sitting on the sofa watching the news before work. It was the same old thing; the world was getting crazier every day. The police situation from yesterday wasn't sitting well with me. I had tried to call Raheem, but it went straight to voicemail each time. I picked the remote up and clicked the tv off.

There was a low growl from behind me. It made the hair on the back of my neck stand up. I was too terrified to turn around.

"If you weren't carrying my brother's child, I would rip your fucking head off," Elijah hissed from behind me. The heat rolling off of him felt like hell fire.

I wrapped my arms around my belly. "What have I done?"

The wolf behind me howled.

I finally got the courage to turn around and face him. He was huge. Tall with dark skin and broad shoulders. The hate for me was obvious in his eyes. He wrinkled his nose like he smelled something bad.

"What are you doing here?" I asked.

"Who just hands over someone else's DNA for a blank warrant?" He slammed the piece of paper on the table next to me.

I jumped. Terrified that he would crush every bone in my body.

"I thought they were the police. They had guns," I stuttered. "If they weren't police, then who were they?"

"Someone who already knew about us, and now thanks to you they have my brother," he said.

"What do you mean they have Raheem where?" panic was starting to set in. He didn't answer my question, instead he walked to the front door and looked out of the peephole.

"How did you know I was pregnant? I haven't missed a cycle." I was having a hard time processing the fact that I was pregnant, especially since I had been on the pill since college, never missing a day.

He raised an eyebrow at me and adjusted his jacket. "I can smell your changing hormones."

Why hadn't Raheem known? Or did he know and not say anything? Elijah opened the front door and in walked a tall older lady with mahogany skin, amber eyes, and long silver hair. She was stunning. Behind her were two men. One was young; he couldn't have been more than twenty-one. He was tall and slim with a baby face, dark brown eyes, and curly hair. If it weren't for the tattoos on his neck and face, he would be a pretty boy. The man behind him was medium height and burly. The right side of his face was covered in burn scars. The young one gave me a sympathetic smile, but the other looked at me like I was trash on the sidewalk. And for what I had done to Raheem, I deserved that.

"Lucinda," thanks for getting here so quickly," Elijah said. He walked over and gave her a kiss on both cheeks, and gave each man a quick hug and pat on the back.

Lucinda shot me an evil look. "So you are the one causing all this trouble?"

I looked at the ground, already feeling ashamed.

"You are carrying a son that holds our bloodline, so don't be weak now," she snapped. I was having a son. I had just had the most awkward gender reveal in history, and I didn't feel happy about it. Maybe it was just being in a room full of creatures who wanted to kill me.

The air in the townhouse was thick and musky. I had finally gotten my wish of meeting Raheem's family, and they all hated me. Raheem had trusted me with his most guarded secret, and I blabbed it all without even looking at the warrant, too busy worrying about saving my own butt.

The pack members all walked into the kitchen. The young one opened the fridge and looked around. "Damn, shorty ain't got no food in here." He shut the door and grabbed a bottle of Hennessy. He popped the top and started drinking it straight out of the bottle.

He strolled into the front room and sat in the recliner, putting his feet on my glass dining table. If the situation hadn't been so dire, I would have cussed him out, but I would not push my luck.

"So, what do we do now?" I asked Lucinda as she walked around the sofa.

"There is no *we*. Our pack is going to handle this. We have a protocol for this situation." It did not surprise me that they didn't trust me or try to hide their disdain for me.

"Rocco, we will be right back. Do not let this woman out of your sight. Do you understand?" Elijah said.

"Yea, boss, I got it. She isn't going anywhere."
He had an accent that I had heard before. It was the
same accent my college roommate, Julie, had.

Lucinda, Elijah, and the other man walked out
of the house. I heard a vehicle back out of the
parking lot and speed off.

"You from New Orleans?" I asked.

"Yeah. How did you know?"

"Your accent."

"It always gives me away." He had a sweet
smile. He looked so innocent, it was hard to believe
that there was a killer inside of him.

"How old are you, Rocco?"

"Old enough." He took a swig from the bottle
like he was trying to convince me.

I sat back on the sofa and twirled a lock of hair
around my finger.

"I won't hurt you," he said as he sat the bottle
on the table. " You are carrying Raheem's seed, so
you are basically family." That simple statement hit
me right in the gut.

"I'm really sorry about how this all played out."
I wiped a tear from my cheek.

"It's all good, baby girl; we all mess up sometimes." He shrugged his shoulders.

"You wouldn't believe some of the shit I have gotten myself into, but the pack has never turned its back on me," he said, reaching for the bottle again. "I done had a lot of girl trouble, not to mention I thought I was a hot boy trying to sell dope, but Raheem and Elijah showed me there was a different way. They were like inspiration, showing us, we could own businesses. I have seen Raheem break bread with some of these young cats in his mentor program, buying them school clothes and shoes, so they don't have to hustle.

Hearing Rocco's admiration for Raheem made me tear up again.

Chapter 9

There was a hard knock on the door. The type of knock that only came from the butt end of a flashlight. I had heard it many times in my life when the police had shown up for welfare checks on my mom. Rocco recognized it too, because he sat up and looked at the door. Why in the world were the police here? Was it really the police? After everything that had happened, it was impossible to tell, but I would not risk it again.

Rocco mouthed the word "go" to me and we both stood up. I motioned for him to follow me to the back bedroom.

Then there was a barrage of gunshots. It sounded like they were coming from everywhere. I screamed. Rocco put a hand around my mouth and pulled me to the floor. He laid his body on top of mine. Rocco flinched and groaned as the bullets flew into him.

The shooting stopped. Car doors slammed and tires screeched as they pulled away. I laid still for a few more seconds, barely breathing, just to make sure they were gone.

"Rocco, are you okay?" It was a stupid question, but it was the only thing I could get out.

He was bleeding, and smoke was coming out of the bullet holes.

"Silver!" he groaned. I thought werewolves could heal themselves, but that wasn't happening. I panicked. I didn't know what to do.

"Rocco, we got to get outta here; whoever did that might come back."

"Leave me here, Yolanda!" he whispered.

There was no way in hell I was leaving him here. He had just saved my life.

"Come on, Rocco. Hold on to me." He wrapped his arm around my shoulder, and I lifted him. Even though Rocco was skinny, he was still heavy. We inched toward the front door.

A cell phone buzzed in his back pocket. I reached into his pocket and pulled the phone out.

Rocco wasn't looking good. The color was fading from his face, and his eyes were barely opened. If he passed out, there was no way I could carry him.

I opened the phone.

"Rocco? Rocco?" It was Lucinda. There was panic in her voice. I was still dragging him out of the house and onto the porch.

"Somebody just shot up the house. Rocco got hit; he's alive but slipping."

Lucinda didn't say anything. There was only the click of the phone.

We were almost down the porch stairs when the black SUV pulled up. The passenger door flew open. Lucinda ran over and picked Rocco up like he weighed as much as a feather.

"Come on, or get left!" she hollered over her shoulder. She climbed into the backseat with Rocco. I ran as fast as I could. I was out of breath when I climbed into the front seat and slammed the door shut. Elijah hit the gas, and we were gone.

I looked in the backseat as Lucinda ripped off Rocco's cargo pants.

"Why isn't he healing?" I asked.

She just shook her head and kept looking at him over. she stuck her finger in one of the wounds and dug around.

Rocco cried out in pain.

"I'm sorry, baby." She pulled out a silver casing. It smoked as it burned her hands. She dropped it immediately. "Silver."

Lucinda did the same thing for the rest of his wounds. There were five silver bullets in all. The pained sounds coming from Rocco made me want to put my hand over my ears like a little kid. Instead, I sat there and watched in horror.

"Is he going to be, okay?"

Lucinda's hands were covered in blood. "I don't know. The silver got into his bloodstream."

"Who would have weapons equipped with silver?"

Elijah growled and punched the steering wheel. "The same people that have Raheem." Something crashed into the back of us with a long bang. I flew forward and smacked my head on the dashboard. I looked out the rearview mirror. There was a jacked-up truck with some type of bar grill on the front."

"Elijah, we got trouble," I said.

"Obviously!" he yelled. The truck sped up behind us, but had a hard time keeping up. Elijah threw his cell phone at me.

"Call contact number nine and tell him to activate code black."

"What's code black?"

"Yolanda, just fucking do it!"

The truck rammed us again. I dropped the phone and scrambled to pick it up off the floorboard. My hands were shaking so badly I had a hard time holding on to the phone. I found the contact and pressed the call button. It rang one time.

"Hello? Hello? Activate code black."

No one said anything, but the line went dead.

Elijah weaved in and out of traffic, trying to lose this truck, but whoever was driving it was determined. Elijah swung a wild turn onto an exit, and the truck swung right behind us.

There was a red light coming up. If we had to stop, that truck was going to be on us in no time. Lucinda was holding on to Rocco tight. He wasn't moving. I thought I was going to puke, but I swallowed it back down.

I looked back at the truck following us. A man was hanging out of the passenger side window. I could see he was holding something long and black.

"Elijah, he's got a gun!" I screamed as the back window shattered.

Our SUV slammed into the car in front of us. Glass went everywhere, and the airbags deployed, punching me in the face. There was a barrage of gunfire. All I could do was put my hands over my head and duck.

The doors to the truck popped open. Someone was trying to pull me out of the truck. I was swinging my hands, beating whoever it was taking me.

"Yolanda, stop fighting." It was Elijah. He was dragging me into the backseat of another SUV. When I opened my eyes, two bodies were lying next to the truck we had just gotten out of.

The doors shut, and we sped away. Me and Lucinda were in the backseat Rocco was laid across her lap. There were cuts on her cheeks and around her eyes.

"Are you okay?"

"Just glass," she said without even looking at me.

The burned man was driving, and Elijah was on the passenger side. The SUV floated down the highway. There was a black truck in front of us t and another behind us. I assumed they were other werewolves; part of a safety convoy. Our truck driver hooked a right, and we started down a rural road. The truck in front and the one behind us kept going.

We drove down a rocky road of dirt and gravel. We went for a while before we stopped in front of a cabin surrounded by trees. The doors to the truck flew open and everybody jumped out.

The two men carried Rocco into the house. Lucinda was right behind them. They all went into a backroom and shut the door.

I sat down on an old recliner and pulled my feet up. I hoped Rocco was okay, and I prayed that wherever Raheem was, he was okay too.

I had opened Pandora's box.

I rubbed my belly again and wished he would flutter for me. But he stayed still.

Chapter 10

Lucinda came out of the back room. She had cleaned the blood from her face, and her scratches had healed up. She sat down on the sofa

"How is Rocco?"

"He needs to change so his body can heal. The silver is going to make his change painful, but it's the only way." She leaned back on the sofa and closed her eyes.

"Do you have any idea who did this?"

She shook her head. "Whoever it is has been preparing for a long time. There's no way they got this organized out the blue."

The rest of the day dragged by. It was tense as we waited for the sun to go down.

When it was time, Elijah walked out of the bedroom carrying Rocco; he was limp and lifeless, his arms and legs dangled. I held back the tears because those bullets had been meant for me.

I followed them outside. Elijah laid Rocco on the ground next to the fire pit. Elijah and the other man shifted. No matter how many times I saw it happen, I just couldn't get over it. It looked so painful, but when it was over, they were so powerful.

I wondered if the baby I was carrying would shift, or if he would stay in human form. Thinking of my future child as something other than human was an odd feeling.

Me and Raheem had never talked about having babies. We were being safe, so I never thought it would be an issue. But apparently, the pill was no match for his super sperm.

Lucinda was a beautiful werewolf; her silver fur was sleek. She walked over to Rocco and kneeled down. She cradled him in her arms and licked his face and howled. Elijah and the other wolf joined in. It was heartbreaking.

Rocco's feet twitched—and then his hands.

"Come on, Rocco. You got this," I whispered.

The twitching got steadier; Lucinda laid him back on the ground.

His body jerked, and then he was up on his knees. He tossed his head back. As his yellow eyes glowed, he whimpered and whined, and then he changed. Rocco's wolf was sandy red. The three other wolves all howled and ran off toward the woods. Lucinda stopped and looked back at me. She growled and pointed a paw toward the cabin. Great. I was being told to go inside like a child.

Two hours later, it was Elijah who walked in the door first, followed by Rocco, Lucinda, and the mystery man.

I ran up to Rocco and wrapped my arms around him.

"I'm so glad you're okay."

"It's all good; ya boy made it through." I could tell he wasn't feeling a hundred percent, but he was definitely on the mend.

"Thanks again for saving me back at the house."

"Every member of this pack would lay down their life for that baby you are carrying," Lucinda cut in. It wasn't lost on me she excluded me from the equation. I went back to my chair to nurse my hurt feelings.

Elijah sat on the couch. I could see the resemblance between him and Raheem in the facial structure, but that was it. Elijah looked harder. I couldn't imagine him smiling or cracking a joke. But I guess if you were the alpha of the pack, you had to be hard when the survival of your entire family rested on your shoulders.

"I have a contact inside the hospital. He says that Raheem is there. Apparently, there is a heavy military presence and doctors are running tests on him." My heart broke thinking of him being treated like some type of guinea pig.

"Yo Elijah, who are these people?" Rocco asked.

"I'm going to get to the bottom of it but first we need to get Raheem out of that hospital

If they take him to some type of black site, we might never get him back." First thing in the morning, we will make a plan. There won't be any time for mistakes. I fear our normal office has been compromised, but we should be able to scrape up everything we need. The rest of the pack is scattered throughout the city, waiting for orders. I have a connection who works in the police station. They are running the prints from one of the guys that ran us off the road earlier. He's going to get back to me with the information."

"Elijah, how do you have so many contacts in all these places?" I asked.

"When your life depends on staying hidden, you learn how to leverage information."

"And humans," Lucinda added.

Elijah looked at me. "There's another room back there. You can sleep there for the night."

I nodded my head and went to the room. Once again, I was being dismissed.

I walked into the bedroom. There was a twin sized bed and a little night stand. That was it. I shut the door behind me and undressed. I laid on the stiff mattress, but I couldn't relax.

Never get him back rang over and over in my head. That thought was too much for me to bear. He had to come home; he had a son to raise. If he never forgave me, I would understand. Because I wasn't sure if I could forgive myself.

The others were whispering in the front room. I wondered what they were talking about, but eventually, that too got quiet. I closed my eyes. All I could think about was Raheem and how kind he had been to me and how it had gone down the drain because I couldn't have my fairytale family. I flopped around, but eventually, sleep came for me.

Chapter 11

The next morning, I walked out of the bedroom. Everyone else was already sitting around the table. No one except Rocco looked my way.

"Good morning, Yolanda," he said when he saw me walking out of the room.

"Morning Rocco.

Elijah had a map spread out on the table.

"Raheem is in here." He tapped at a point on the map. It was marked *laboratory*. "The goal is to get in and get him out without too much attention, but if we have to fight our way out, so be it."

Rocco was tapping his leg. He looked like he was back to his full strength, which made me happy. The quiet one was hanging on to every word Elijah said. Lucinda looked bored, but she still shot daggers at me.

"What do you need me to do" I asked

"Nothing," Lucinda and Elijah said in unison. Rocco grinned and shook his head.

"First of all, I'm the only human, AND I'm pregnant. So, what better way to get into the hospital undetected?"

"Technically, any of us can get into the hospital," Lucinda said.

"Yeah, but if they take your blood before you get a room, the charade is up."

"She's got a point," Rocco said.

Lucinda rolled her eyes, and Elijah tensed up. But as much as they wanted me to sit in this cabin and be the scared little human, it wasn't happening. I cared about Raheem, too. Elijah rubbed his temples before he looked up at me.

"Once you get inside, you need to get eyes on Raheem and then call us. We will go in and extract him. Our man on the inside said they have one or two guards walking around, carrying some heavy artillery."

I sat back in the chair. Did I really want to do this, or was I just trying to poke my chest out and make them respect me? I could hold my own, but this wasn't some street fight or some young girl popping off at me in the middle of the night. Whoever had Raheem was out for blood, and I'm sure they wouldn't mind spilling some of mine if it came down to it.

An hour later, we were coasting down the highway, almost to the hospital.

"You good, Yolanda?" Rocco asked

I smiled and nodded, but I wanted to scream and tell them to pull over and let me out of this damn truck. He put his hand on mine and squeezed. I had to blink back the tears. It was amazing how a little act of kindness really felt. If this was the type of love that came from the pack, I was glad my son would have it, even if it left me on the outside looking in.

When we pulled up to the hospital, Elijah unbuckled his seatbelt and turned to look at me in the backseat.

"Yolanda Try not to fuck this up." he said as he handed me a cellphone.

Chapter 12

I closed the truck's door, adjusted my shirt, and walked through the hospital's sliding doors. A few people were in the small waiting room. The receptionist was behind a glass shield. The sounds of people coughing and crying were unnerving, but it was a hospital, so what did I expect? I looked around. I had been expecting people in hazmat suits holding guns like in the zombie movies, but nothing in here looked suspicious.

I walked up to the receptionist. She looked like she would rather be anywhere else.

"How can I help you?"

"I'm pregnant and having some cramps and spotting." I thought it might garner some emotion from her, but it didn't. She just slid a clipboard under the shield.

"Fill this out and bring it back."

Damn, were people really walking around that jaded?

I took the clipboard and sat in one of the hard chairs. I used all fake information, including the name Brittany Johnson, just in case anything went left. I took the clipboard back to the desk.

"Do you have your insurance card?"

"I don't have insurance."

The heffa behind the desk rolled her eyes like somehow an uninsured pregnant woman was an insult to her. If I hadn't been on a mission to rescue Raheem, I would have given her a piece of my mind. People are coming to the hospital sick and scared, and this bitch got an attitude problem. This is one of the things that keeps my clients from getting help.

After taking a deep breath, I went back to my seat. I sat for a while and looked around. I watched as other patients got called to the back.

The cellphone Elijah gave me beeped.

"Anything...?"

"Still waiting." Did they not understand you couldn't just walk up and demand to see a doctor?

A curvy nurse with her hair in a bun came out holding a clipboard. "Brittany Johnson?"

That's when it clicked; she was calling me. I stood up and followed her past the double doors. She showed me to a room, and I sat at the table.

"How far along are you?" she asked as she checked my blood pressure.

I hadn't even thought about that question. Being pregnant still felt surreal, especially since I didn't get to experience the usual scenario of realizing my period was late.

"I'm not sure. I just got the positive test today, and a few hours later, I started spotting."

She shook her head and gave me a little half smile that let me know she understood. She wrote on her notepad and walked out.

I was sitting there, trying to figure out what I was supposed to do next. A loud alarm started blaring. It scared the hell out of me. I jumped off the table and opened the door to see what was going on. Nurses and doctors were walking out of the rooms. A few of them were escorting patients to the exits. Everyone looked confused. Maybe they thought it was some type of fire drill. I knew it would be in this confusion that I could go look for Raheem. I took out the phone and shot Elijah a text—*Alarm, everyone leaving.*

I walked out of the room and blended right in with everyone else. I made a few turns and wondered where in the heck the lab was. A man in a green pair of scrubs was walking past me. "Sir, could you tell me where the lab is?"

"Go straight down the hall and then make a right. Can't miss it." The halls were thinning out, so I needed to move quickly. I followed the man's directions. Luckily, the door was already propped open, so I just slipped inside. There was a row of long tables and desks. There were three men, all at a table. They all had their backs to me. One of them was wearing a lab coat and the other two had on camo, and they were holding enormous guns. I slipped under one of the desks.

"This is unbelievable. The cells are reattaching themselves! Just imagine what we could do if all our soldiers could heal themselves. We have spent years trying to find these creatures, but they have been able to hide in plain sight. We have to collect more samples."

There was another, deeper voice. "We sent a team to retrieve them, but they got away.

"No, you idiots sent a hit squad. I need the specimens alive; we already lost one on the table, the sedation was too strong."

"I believe we can reverse the silver allergy, and then they would be unstoppable."

I put a hand on my mouth so I wouldn't scream. Oh, God. They had killed my Raheem while trying to create some type of super soldier.

"Dr. Roberts, we just received word that the biologist is here. The chopper just landed."

"Make sure all the civilians are out of the building. We need to get samples from the specimen we still have left. He's not looking too good; I'm not sure he will survive a helicopter ride. Even though these creatures are strong and have amazing regenerative power, they are sensitive to sedation."

A chill ran up my spine. The three men walked out of the lab. I stayed hidden until I was sure they were gone. I shot Elijah a text *in the lab.*

I walked over to where the two-armed guards had been, and there was Raheem. Tied to a chair. There were sensors attached to his head and chest, all connected to a bunch of monitors.

"Raheem. Wake up, baby."

His head was drooping. He moaned. I ripped the connectors from his head. The machines beeped. I had to get out of here before anyone came to investigate.

"Raheem, honey, it's me. I need you to get up." I untied the ropes that held him to the chair.

"Yolanda..." It came out like a whisper.

"Yes, baby. It's me, I need you to get up."

He tried to get up, but fell back down. I put his arm over my shoulder and hoisted him up. It took all the strength I could muster. We shuffled out the door and into the hallway. We were just a few steps away from the elevator.

"Stop!" someone yelled from behind us. Then, the whizz of bullets as they hit the walls and the floor around us.

"Stop, you idiots! I need him alive," the doctor yelled at them.

Raheem was waking up, but he was still groggy. We got on the elevator before they could reach us. When we stepped into the lobby, a group of soldiers was coming down the stairs.

"Stop!" they commanded. This was it. We had been so close. I could see the door from here. But I knew if we ran, they would shoot, even though the doctor had warned them not to.

"Turn around now!"

Raheem's eyes flickered between yellow and brown. But I knew there wasn't much he could do, especially since the soldiers had silver artillery. I had seen the damage it did to Rocco. We turned around and looked at the soldiers.

"Come towards us now."

There was a growl and then another one.

"What the hell is that?" one soldier asked as they looked around, trying to figure out which way the threat was coming from.

The werewolves were blurs, moving around in the shadows.

One soldier let off a shot, and the wolves pounced.

The sounds of snarling and snapping was loud in the lobby. I watched in horror as arms, legs, and other body parts flew around us. I grabbed Raheem and started toward the door. Even though the wolves had this under control, I knew there were more soldiers on the way, and they would be here any second. I got us out of the door and into the parking lot. The sun blinded me for a second, but I saw Elijah as he ran up to us in wolf form, his fur matted with blood. He grabbed Raheem and ran toward the waiting SUV.

"Yolanda, over here." Rocco pulled up beside me in a black SUV. I jumped in and he peeled out of the parking lot before I could shut the door.

"Thanks, Rocco," I said as I tried to catch my breath.

His eyes were wild, and he was smiling, but he didn't look so innocent this time. There was blood smeared across his face.

"Rocco, I'm starting to think you're like my guardian angel or something."

He smiled. "I'm your Pack angel...that has a nice ring to it."

I shook my head.

The truck sped down the highway. Rocco kept looking back, making sure that no one was following us. We exited off toward the cabin. We both jumped out of the truck and ran inside the cabin. The back bedroom door was open, Raheem was laying down. His eyes were barely open, and he was breathing hard. Elijah was at his side, holding his hand.

"Will he be, okay?" I asked as I made my way inside.

"They pumped him full of some type of sedative," he said. This was the first time I had seen any type of real emotion from Elijah. He looked worried as he stared at his little brother lying on the bed.

The doctor wanted to extract his DNA; I don't think he would have risked silver getting into his bloodstream.

"Doctor?" he asked. I gave him the rundown about the super soldier plans the Doctor had. "Elijah, Dr. Roberts is determined. It won't be long before they find us out here, and then what are we going to do?"

I'm going to call in the rest of the pack. We lost a few members at the hospital, but the ones left will fight."

"Wouldn't it be better to just run away? Go somewhere safe?"

"Yolanda, whoever that doctor works for will never stop chasing us."

I shook my head because I knew he was right.

I pulled a chair closer to the bed. I took Raheem's hand. I sat there for a long time, just listening to him breathe.

"Yolanda?"

I sat up. "Raheem. Are you okay?"

"Yes, I'm fine." He was still weak and whispering. I sat on the bed next to him and kissed him on the cheek. He was trying to sit up, so I helped by putting a few pillows behind him. His eyes were low, but I was happy he was alive. "Elijah told me you were pregnant." He put his hand on my belly and smiled. I tried to hide the fact that I was disappointed about not delivering the news myself.

"So, it's a boy, huh?" His tongue was heavy.

"Yes." I put my hand on top of his, and we sat like that for a while.

The door opened, and Lucinda walked in. She had a gnarly cut on her arm, but I could tell it was already healing.

"Raheem." She ran over and wrapped him in a hug. Elijah was right behind her. I got off the bed and stood back.

"Damn, little bro. I thought you were going lay there forever," Elijah said as he walked over to his brother. They embraced one another.

"Raheem, what the hell happened?" Elijah asked.

Raheem cleared his throat. "I got pulled over when I was leaving Yolanda's. The cop acted really weird from the time he pulled me over. He said I had warrants, but instead of taking me to jail, he took me to the hospital. I sat there waiting for a few hours, and then Dr. Roberts and his team showed up. They flashed some papers at me and said I was a national security threat and couldn't call anyone. They started running all types of tests and drawing my blood. They gave me a big ass needle full of medicine, and after that I don't remember much." Lucinda was stroking his hand.

That reminded me of something.

"Raheem, when we were in the lab, the doctor said they had another werewolf. Do you know who it was?" Everyone looked at me like they'd forgotten I was even in the room.

"Yeah, they had a young wolf from a different city, but he couldn't handle all the shit they kept pumping into him." I swallowed the lump in my throat.

"When he died, it pissed them off they had *wasted* their medicine, not that they had killed somebody." Raheem's eyes glowed yellow. I was sorry for making him relive such a painful memory.

Elijah's phone buzzed. "Give me a few. I'm going to sort this out."

He stormed out of the room.

"Raheem, I knew the night they brought you to me that you were a fighter, so I knew you were going to pull through, but you need some rest," Lucinda said.

"I know, Lu. I'm going to talk to Yolanda for a few, and then I will rest, I promise." Lucinda nodded and kissed him on the cheek. She walked out of the room and closed the door. I walked over to his side. He smiled up at me. I took his hand in mine.

"I'm so sorry," I said. And just like that, the floodgates opened.

He squeezed my hand. "It's not your fault, Yolanda." He kissed my hand and closed his eyes. A few moments later he was snoring.

Chapter 13

When I walked into the front room, Rocco and Lucinda were sitting on the sofa. Rocco was staring off into space and Lucinda was stroking her hair. The gash on her arm had completely healed. I sat in the chair and wondered what we were supposed to do next. We sat there in silence for at least an hour.

Elijah rushed in holding a manilla envelope.

"Our contact at the police station came through. It's worse than I thought." The door to the bedroom opened and Raheem stepped out. He was walking, taking steady, strong steps. He walked over and stood beside me.

Elijah opened the folder and started thumbing through the paperwork. There were lots of pictures, some old black and white photographs. Then there was a face I recognized.

"Hey, that's Dr. Roberts from the lab," Raheem said, picking up a photo.

"What is all this, Elijah?" Rocco asked.

Elijah looked like he was struggling to stay calm. I swear his hands were shaking. If this was enough to scare Elijah, then I wasn't sure I wanted to know.

"This shit goes back to World War II. Apparently, Hitler was obsessed with the paranormal. He even created this investigative squad that would go out and investigate anything that even sounded vaguely connected to the paranormal, and then they would arrest the people, but it was really an excuse to run experiments on them. They killed hundreds of humans, but they also discovered some of our ancestors." He flipped to an old black and white sketch of a werewolf mid-shift.

Elijah rubbed his hand over his head. "It gets worse, though. Look." He held up a grainy photo of a group of men with their hands tied up, looking at the ground. There were two soldiers behind them, smiling. "It wasn't just Hitler. In Vietnam, the U.S. troops found a group of werewolves." He showed us another photo. It was a naked man in a silver dog collar chained to a wall.

"His hands," Lucinda whispered. I leaned in closer. There were three bloody stumps where his fingers should have been.

"They would cut off their limbs to watch them heal, over and over again," Elijah said.

"My goodness," I gasped. Raheem put a hand on my shoulder.

Elijah pulled out a stack of transcripts; some of the lines were blacked out. I scanned through the documents. They were accounts of experiments and studies they had run on the werewolves. were pictures of the shifters naked, with probes all over their bodies. The last picture was a man with a collar on and in front of him was a man tied up with his hands behind back.

"They had even been forced to feed on some of their captured POWs." Elijah's eyes glowed yellow but he shook it off.

"So, of course, when this sick shit got out to the public, the government tried to sweep it under the rug. The rumors caused most of the weres to go deep underground. Most packs even stopped having babies because it was too big of a risk. They would sterilize their girls in childhood. They thought it was better to die out than to risk getting captured. But it was too late—the agency knew we were out there, and they started keeping track of any type of activity they thought might be associated with weres—sightings, witness accounts, or strange murders. It was only a matter of time before they found us. They have been biding their time, waiting and getting ready. They don't want to exterminate us; they want to use us for whatever sick twisted thing they can come up with"

"Elijah, I would rather die than be anybody's guinea pig." Rocco said.

"Yeah, man, we can't let that happen." Elijah turned to me. "And if they find out that you're carrying Raheem's child, you can't imagine the hell they would put you through."

My blood ran cold. I knew he wasn't exaggerating.

This time, I couldn't hold it in. I ran outside and puked up everything that was in my stomach. I wiped my mouth with the back of my hand and sat on the porch. I had heard enough. I'm a counselor and every day, I am reminded that evil is real. But this was some next-level darkness. I had never been so afraid in my life.

The door opened, and I turned to look. It was Lucinda. She sat on the porch next to me.

"Have you ever seen anything like this?" I asked

She gave me a half smile. "Yolanda, if anybody can lead us through this thing, it's Elijah. She stood up. "You wanted in, so welcome to the family," she said as she walked back into the cabin.

Raheem walked over to me. He rubbed my back, and I leaned into him.

"I can't believe that people can be that damn evil," I said, trying not to get choked up.

"I'm sorry you had to see that, Yolanda."

"Raheem, I'm sorry, I shouldn't be making this about me; those are your ancestors."

"Since we were young, we have been told about how dangerous the humans were, but I never knew just how bad it was." He pulled me close to him, and for a minute I felt like everything was going to be ok.

There was a loud crashing sound that came from somewhere close. Everyone ran out of the house and stood on the porch.

"Alright, it's time," Elijah said.

Raheem took me by the hand "Yolanda, it's not safe for you here, and it might not be safe on the road, either. If we are not back in an hour, get the hell out of here and don't go home." He pulled me into a hug and kissed me on the mouth, then he shifted, the rest of the pack following suit. They all ran off the porch and into the woods. Not one of them looked back, not even Raheem.

Them going out there seemed like such a bad idea; did they even really have a plan? Or was this some type of suicide mission? I had seen the damage caused by the soldiers' silver ammunition. I walked back into the house. I was completely useless, so I just paced around waiting and glancing out of the blinds every five minutes. When an hour had passed, I walked out on the porch. I knew Raheem had told me to leave, but I couldn't fathom just leaving them out there. I heard a howl. It was the same heartbreaking sound Lucinda had made when Rocco was trying to shift. I took off toward the woods. I walked as quietly as I could. I saw lights and heard voices, but it didn't sound like any of the pack members. I hid behind a tree.

There was a clearing in the woods that was lit up by a big spotlight. A big convoy was out there. I spotted Dr. Roberts and a group of soldiers, behind them was the pack; everyone except Elijah. Each member was chained to the person in front of them. They were all in human form, naked and wearing those awful silver collars. Their hands were tied behind their backs and silver shackles on their feet made it hard for them to walk. One soldier walked up to Lucinda and smacked her on the behind. She lunged at him. The soldier stumbled back and fell down. The rest of the soldiers laughed at him; he pulled something out of his pocket. It looked like a round kitchen timer.

He turned the dial, and suddenly all the pack members fell to their knees and withered in pain. "Not so funny now, is it you bitch?" the soldier yelled. He turned the dial the other way, and all the pack members stood up.

The spotlight went out. All the soldiers looked around. "What the hell..."

And then there was snarling and snapping. The soldiers cried out, and some fired shots at the shadows. The light flickered on and off. I could see flashes of horror. I saw a soldier walking slowly. He was hunched over. Blood was coming out of his mouth as he tried to keep his intestines from spilling out.

Then there was the whining and howling of wolves in pain and screaming out.

The light came back on, shining. A full view of the bloodbath was front and center.

Hot bile rushed to the back of my throat. Dr. Roberts was holding the dial; he was limping and his left arm seemed broken, but he was alive. The werewolves were laying on the ground, tossing and turning.

I spotted Elijah. He was curled up in a ball, trying to protect himself from whatever the doctor was doing.

The doctor walked over to him and kneeled down. "You must be the alpha. Strong and ruthless. You will be the best soldier."

Elijah snarled at the doctor, but he couldn't get up. The doctor stood over him and kicked him. "You be a good boy now and stop."

Elijah and I didn't see eye to eye, but seeing him treated this way made me sick.

Dr. Roberts grabbed Elijah by the arm and yanked him to his feet. He led him toward the other pack members.

"Don't worry, my pets. I'll be back for you all soon," he laughed.

This was my only chance. Who knew what he would do to them if he got all the wolves to their site? I took a deep breath and crept out of my hiding spot.

I trudged through the blood-slick leaves. I ran behind the doctor and put my arm around his throat, and used my legs to sweep his feet from under him. The element of surprise had definitely been on my side because the doctor fell down hard, dropping the device.

"You fucking bitch," he said. I grabbed the device and turned the dial in the opposite direction, hoping that was the right thing to do. It took a moment, but all the werewolves stood up.

The doctor tried to scoot away, but it was no use.

Elijah snarled and plodded toward the doctor. He grabbed Dr. Roberts by the throat and pressed him up against a tree, and growled in his face. The doctor screamed as Elijah punched him in the chest and ripped his still beating heart out.

I fell to my knees and threw up.

"Yolanda, over here!" Raheem called out. I ran to the pack and tried to free them from their collars.

"There must be a key somewhere in the doctor's pocket," Raheem said. His voice was loud and booming in the night. Thankfully, Elijah came back with it and unlocked everybody.

Raheem wrapped his arms around me. "Baby, I'm so sorry you had to see that."

I buried my head in his chest and cried. They were tears of relief.

Chapter 14

The next day, we were on the highway headed home. I was in the backseat, snuggled against Raheem. Elijah was driving, and Rocco was in the passenger seat. Lucinda had stayed at the campsite.

Elijah had reached out to a politician and told him it would be a shame if pictures of war crimes were released to the public. I swear, not even two hours later, three military convoys had arrived to clean up the mess in the woods. The politician had suggested that it was time for the werewolves to officially come out. The entire exchange was unsettling. Like it's okay to just pick up dozens of human bodies and dispose of them based on a handshake deal.

When we pulled up in front of my house, it felt bittersweet. I was happy to be home, and away from all the fighting and the violence, but the bullet holes in the door and walls were like scars reminding me that I wasn't really safe.

Elijah looked over his shoulder at me. "Yolanda." He nodded. That was as close to a thank you as I would ever get from him, and that was okay. I got out of the truck.

When Rocco got out, he and Raheem gave each other dap and Rocco gave me a hug before he jumped back in the front seat. Raheem wrapped his arm around me, and we walked inside the house together. I made a mental note to call a repairman first thing in the morning.

"If I didn't know any better, I would think Rocco has a crush on you," Raheem said as he shut the front door.

"I kicked my shoes off and walked down the hallway to the bedroom.

"Shut up, Raheem. Rocco is like a baby brother." I threw a pillow at him.

He caught it midair. "Remember what happened last time you threw something at me?"

"Really?" I rolled my eyes.

He walked over and grabbed me by the waist and pulled me into him. We kissed, and I pushed him back on the bed.

It felt so good to have him to myself. I had missed everything about him—his smile, his smell, his presence. I climbed on top of him. He ran his hand up my back, and every part of me tingled. He pulled my shirt over my head and unclasped my bra. He cupped my breasts in his hands and gave them a hard squeeze. He gently nibbled my nipples and then sucked on them softly. I was soaking wet by the time he pulled my jeans off. He eased my panties off and placed wet kisses on my stomach. He slowly kissed the inside of my thighs. I was squirming.

He grabbed me by the hips. "Be still."

He spread my legs and kissed my swollen outside lips, before he spread them open with his tongue. He gently licked my swollen clit before he took it in his mouth and sucked on it gently.

I cried out in pure ecstasy.

He gently slid two fingers inside of me and hooked them forward while he sucked on my clit. The pleasure rolled over me in waves so intense it was almost painful. Suddenly I was overcome with tears; all the emotions I had been feeling over the last few days just exploded and I was sobbing.

"Yolanda, what's wrong? Did I hurt you?"

"Raheem, I'm so sorry about all of this." He pulled me into his arms.

"Baby, it's not your fault. Those people have been tracking us for a long time. I'm glad you gave them what they wanted. They would have killed you." He wiped the tears off my face. "I wasn't being a good partner to you. There was just so much going on with the pack and I couldn't talk to you about it, so the way I moved looked sneaky."

"Did you know I was pregnant before you left?"

"I would have never left if I knew." I believed him and after everything I had been through it felt good to believe in someone.

He grabbed me by the chin and looked me in my eyes.

"Yolanda you are mine." I untangled myself from his arms and stood up.

"Lay back on the bed and let me show you how much I missed you." His eyes lit up, and he did as he was told.

The next morning, I was sprawled across the bed, still glowing from last night. Raheem was next to me, snoring loud as hell. It felt so good. So normal. Raheem's cell phone started buzzing. I tried to ignore it, but whoever it was wasn't getting the hint.

I shook Raheem until he woke up

"Huh, what's going on babe?" he said, startled, as he sat straight up.

"Your phone." I sat up and folded my arms across my chest, feeling major déjà vu.

Raheem dug the phone out of his pants and answered it.

"Hello." I tried to read his face, but I couldn't make out what he was feeling.

"Okay," he said as he hung up the phone." "The council has summoned me."

"What does that mean?" I went from pissed off to nervous in a matter of seconds.

"It's time for me to face my punishment." He got out of bed and started pulling on his clothes.

"Punishment for what?"

"Telling you what I really am."

I screwed my face up. I'd thought all of this was over. "What do you think is going to happen?"

"Probably lashes or being demoted."

I didn't know what to expect, but I knew we were going to face it together.

Chapter 15

We walked into the meeting room. The room was packed. There were members there that I had never seen before. I wondered how many of them had been in the woods fighting. Everyone was dressed formally. Raheem had forgotten to tell me that bit, so I looked out of place in my black leggings and t-shirt. I spotted Rocco. He gave me a little head nod. It was weird to see him stern and not smiling. I couldn't wait to talk to Rocco alone. Me and Raheem planned to ask him to be our son's godfather. I stood by the door since there were no free chairs in the room.

Lucinda and Elijah were sitting at the table.

Raheem walked over and sat in the chair that was in front of the council table.

"Council," he said, as he gave them a nod.

After everything we had been through, it was bizarre to see him address them so formally. But I had to remind myself that this was pack business. Their rules were not the rules I was used to playing by.

Elijah cleared his throat and started talking. "Raheem, as we all know, the organization got your DNA from your human partner." I wanted to crawl into the floor and disappear, but I kept my head up. "It was also revealed that you allowed your human partner to see you in your true form.

"As a member of this pack, you know that secrecy is crucial to our survival. Because of your indiscretions, you put our lives in danger, and they killed several members of the pack. Their blood is on your hands." Raheem was stone faced looking at Elijah. I knew that this was a serious charge, but it seemed like Elijah wasn't giving Raheem any leeway, even though they were brothers.

"The council, in its entirety, has decided that the punishment is exile."

Raheem's eyes bugged out. I put my hand over my mouth. How could they do this to him? Elijah was the alpha; couldn't he step in and do something?

"Raheem, we exclude you and any descendants that you have from all pack business. No member of this pack will be allowed to associate with you, and if they do, they, too, will be exiled."
Raheem jumped out of his chair; it toppled back.

"Damn, Elijah...this is what it's come to?" He kneeled down and growled. The pack behind him all took a few steps closer to him; they would protect Elijah by any means necessary.

I ran over to Raheem and put his hand on my belly.

He shook his head from left to right, and the yellow glow left his eyes.

Elijah motioned for the members to step back. That was the only mercy he was going to give Raheem, and for that, I was grateful.

Elijah adjusted his shirt. "Raheem, say your goodbyes."

Raheem walked over to each member; he shook hands with some and shared hugs with the others. Everyone was trying to look casual, but none of them could hold eye contact for more than a few seconds without getting teary-eyed. It was like a funeral; only the person you were saying goodbye to was still alive. I walked over and gave Rocco a hug. I cried into his shoulder.

"It's okay, baby girl, y'all are free now," he whispered.

"You're still his godfather."

His eyes lit up, and he smiled. "Always."

I pulled away and dried my eyes. Raheem pulled Rocco into a hug. They embraced for a long time.

"Stay dangerous, Rocco."

"I got you, big bro." They were both blinking back tears.

Rocco stepped back and Lucinda walked over. She wrapped her arms around his neck. "Raheem, you have always been a rebel. "Goodbye. Take care of yourself and your family."

I could tell it was taking everything inside of her not to break down. Elijah and Raheem were both like sons to her. She had raised them, and now she had to say goodbye to one of them. She released him. His eyes were glassy.

"I will." Raheem was choked up.

Everyone walked out of the room, leaving Elijah and Raheem.

I waited at the door. Both of them just stared at each other. There was no hug, no embrace, nothing. They nodded at each other. And that was it.

Raheem walked up beside me and took my hand.

When we got outside, all of the other wolves were lined up against the wall with their backs to him. Including Lucinda. Raheem held his head up high, but tears were falling down his face. We walked out of the building and climbed into the truck. He slammed the door, and we sped away from the building. I couldn't even look at him.

I had taken him away from his only family, his traditions, and his ancestry. I had never felt lower in my life. We were quiet the entire ride home.

When we pulled into the driveway, he turned and looked at me." Yolanda, I can't handle being in the same city so close to the pack." I couldn't imagine how hard it would be to know your family was only a few blocks away, yet you couldn't speak to them. How heartbreaking would it be to walk past your mother figure and she turned her head away like she didn't know you.

He ran a hand across his head.

"Baby, let's load up, get in the car and start over somewhere new with our son."

I was surprised and flustered. "Where would we go, Raheem?"

"I got a nice bit of savings; we can go anywhere you want." he said.

I thought about the shelter and my momma. I hadn't seen her in a while, but it was going to be hard to be so far away from her. I hesitated. I hadn't been expecting to have to make this type of decision. Raheem had lost his entire life and family because of my bullshit, and he was still rocking with me.

I looked up into his eyes. I knew he would never lead me astray. He would protect me and my son from anything, and at that moment, I vowed to do the same.

"Let's hit the road," I said.

We got out of the truck and walked inside the house. I must have lost my mind agreeing to just up and move, with no plan and a baby on the way.

Raheem pulled me into a hug and then he pulled away. He got on one knee. "Yolanda, I want to know if you would do me the honor of being my wife. Me and you against the world."

My damn eyes went cross. I couldn't believe he was really here, proposing to me.

"Yes! Yes, I'll be your wife."

He jumped up and spun me around. " We will grab you a ring when we get settled."

I was smiling hard, probably showing every tooth in my head, because I couldn't believe this was happening to me. I knew one day he might blame me for being exiled, but I knew we could work through it together.

A few hours later, we were packed up. We had only grabbed our clothes and shoes. I called and planned for movers to box everything else up. We decided that when we got settled, we would contact a real estate agent to work on getting the house up for sale.

We were in the truck, backing out of the driveway. I took one last look at the house. I was going to miss this place. I had bought it on my own; it was something I was proud of, but I didn't have to be tethered to it.

"Baby, do you mind if we stop by the shelter so I can say goodbye to everyone?"

"Of course not."

I pulled out my phone and tried to dial my momma. It rang once and went straight to voicemail. I dropped the phone back in my purse.

"You, okay?" he asked.

"I'm good," I said as I looked at him, my love, my future."

Some people say love is a bitch, but I say love is a beast, but he's mine, and I'm going to stick beside him.

The End

Heir of Exile is the next book in the series get your copy today!

Want more Yolanda and Raheem? Join my community and get an exclusive scene that was too hot for the book!

https://dl.bookfunnel.com/hkpb6ascyp

www.ingramcontent.com/pod-product-compliance
Lightning Source LLC
Chambersburg PA
CBHW010321180726
47991CB00022B/3165